The Family Squeeze

Words by Christian Pulcini
Art by Matthew Gauvin

Burlington, Vermont

Text Copyright © 2024 by Christian Pulcini

Illustration Copyright © 2024 by Matthew Gauvin

All rights reserved. No part of this publication may be reproduced, distributed, or transmitted in any form or by any means, including photocopying, recording, or other electronic or mechanical methods, without the prior written permission of the publisher, except in the case of brief quotations embodied in critical reviews and certain other noncommercial uses permitted by copyright law.

Onion River Press
Burlington, VT 05401
info@onionriverpress.com
www.onionriverpress.com

ISBN: 978-1-957184-65-4

Library of Congress Control Number: 2024913367

Dedicated to the creators of the family squeeze - Nicole, Juliette, Henry, and Alice.

There is nothing quite like a family squeeze...
(SQUEEZE!)

Family squeeze
for when you are new

Family squeeze
for when you are few

Family squeeze for when you are more

Family squeeze for when you go out the door

Family squeeze for when you fall

Family squeeze for when you score the ball

Family squeeze for when you ride a bike

Family squeeze for things you don't like

Family squeeze for when you dream

Family squeeze
for when you scream

Family squeeze
for when you drive a car

Family squeeze
for when you become a star

Family squeeze
for when things are sad

Family squeeze
for when things are glad

Family squeeze
for when you say please

Family squeeze
for when you say cheese

Family squeeze for strength you need

Family squeeze
for the path you lead

Family squeeze for when you roam

Family squeeze
for when you come home

Family squeeze for when you walk with grace

Family squeeze for when you glow

Family squeeze for when you grow

Family squeeze
for those who are new

Family squeeze for new traditions, too

Family squeeze for all shapes and sizes

Because there is nothing quite like a family squeeze...
(SQUEEZE!)

Christian D. Pulcini, MD, MEd, MPH lives in Vermont and is a pediatric emergency physician and researcher focused on children with disabilities, children's mental health/trauma, and firearm injuries. He is also a former middle school science teacher. This is Christian's first published book, and the inspiration for it can be entirely attributed to his wonderful family of 5 and their loving family squeezes.

Matthew Gauvin was born in Vermont and spent five years in Boston studying at Massachusetts College of Art and Design where he graduated with a BFA in Illustration. He has since illustrated around thirty books and has worked on projects ranging from logo design to pet portraits, magazines, CDs, and his work was displayed in various galleries, festivals, fairs and private collections around the U.S. He has received various national and international awards for his art and recently launched a new art venture with a focus on landscape painting under the name "Edge of Nature Studio".

Printed in the USA
CPSIA information can be obtained
at www.ICGtesting.com
CBHW062328230824
13640CB00012B/129